TOM and JERRY™

THE CHEESE MAKING MOUSE

Written by Bill Matheny
Illustrated by ComicUp!

Book design by John Sazaklis

First published in this format in 2015 by Curious Fox,
an imprint of Capstone Global Library Limited,
7 Pilgrim Street, London, EC4V 6LB
– Registered company number: 6695582
www.curious-fox.com

CAPG34400

Originated by Capstone Global Library Ltd
Printed and bound in Slovakia by TBB

ISBN 978-1-782-02277-0
18 17 16 15 14
10 9 8 7 6 5 4 3 2 1

A CIP catalogue record for this book is available
from the British Library.

The National Literacy Trust is a registered charity no: 1116260 and a company limited by guarantee no. 5836486
registered in England and Wales and a registered charity in Scotland no. SC042944. Registered address: 68 South
Lambeth Road, London SW8 1RL.
National Literacy Trust logo and reading tips © National Literacy Trust 2014
www.literacytrust.org.uk/donate

"Hmm..." said Tom, as he stood on the front porch. Someone has left Jerry a package. Tom wants to know what's inside so he decides to open it.

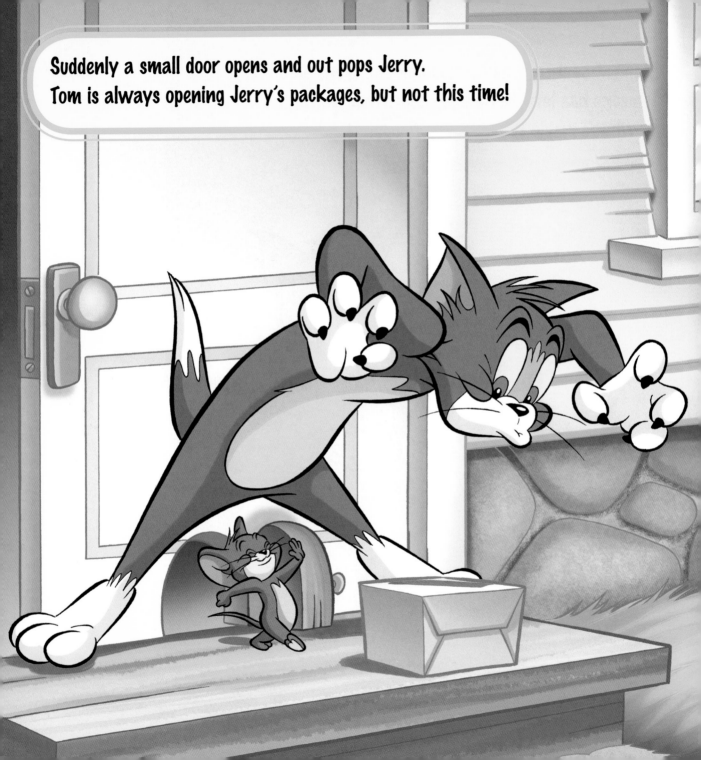

Suddenly a small door opens and out pops Jerry.
Tom is always opening Jerry's packages, but not this time!

Jerry grabs his package before Tom can do anything.
The cat is so surprised, that he doesn't even wave back.

Jerry's nephew, Tuffy, can't believe it. A cheese making kit of their very own!
Now they can make any flavour cheese they want, from chocolate to pizza!
"I'm hungry now, Uncle Jerry!" says Tuffy. "Can we get started?"
Jerry nods. It's time to make some cheese!

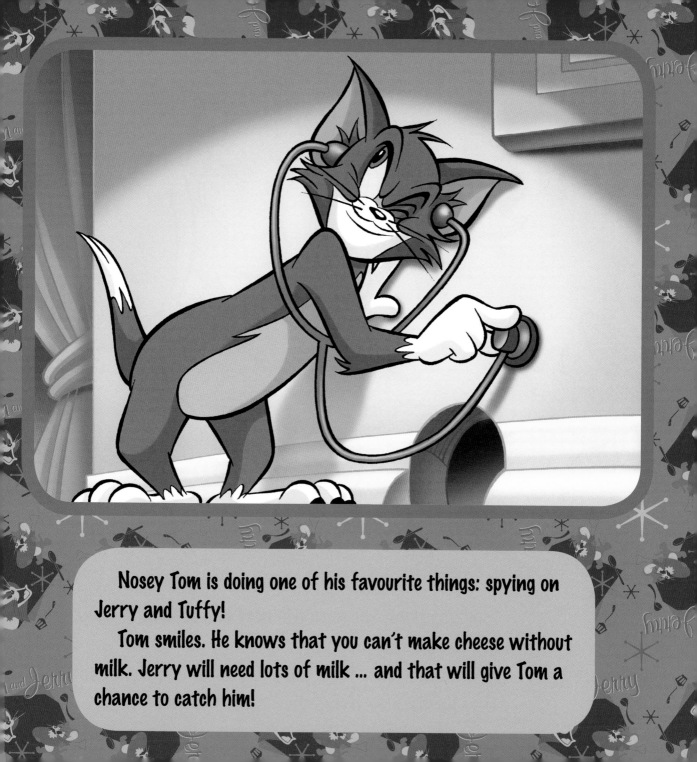

Nosey Tom is doing one of his favourite things: spying on Jerry and Tuffy!

Tom smiles. He knows that you can't make cheese without milk. Jerry will need lots of milk ... and that will give Tom a chance to catch him!

Tom was right. The mice will need lots of milk to make their cheese.

At the farm, they have some fun while Tom chases them. They have a new friend they want Tom to meet.

Uh oh! Jerry's new friend isn't happy to meet Tom.
Tom races across the field with the snorting bull hot on his tail.
"Good thinking, Uncle Jerry," says Tuffy. "That lazy old cat needs some exercise!"

Jerry has made his first batch of cheese and wants to share it with Tom.

"Be careful, Uncle Jerry!" warns Tuffy. Jerry isn't scared.

Tom watches Jerry walk out of his mouse hole wearing a special suit, but he doesn't care.

He wants the mouse, not the cheese!

When Tom pounces on Jerry, he is surprised that the mouse doesn't try to escape.

Tuffy gasps, "Oh no, Uncle Jerry's in trouble!"

But, wait a minute... Tom smells something funny. It's Jerry's triple garlic and onion cheese!

Tom sniffs the air a couple of times, then gets a funny look on his face.
"Ohhhhh...!" The strong smell of the cheese has made Tom pass out.
   "Great work, Uncle Jerry!" cheers Tuffy. "Some stinky cheese for a stinky cat!"
Tom won't be catching any mice today. He's too busy catnapping.

Jerry doesn't want Tom to miss the party. He and Tuffy decide to wake him up.
"One ... two ... three ... Pull!" says Tuffy.
"Mee-Ouch!" cries Tom as he springs up and rubs his whiskers. That hurt!

Jerry has a lot of hungry friends in the neighbourhood. It doesn't
take long before the word gets out: "Free cheese at Jerry's house!"
All the mice are eager to taste more of Jerry's homemade cheese.
"Don't forget your crackers!" Tuffy reminds them.

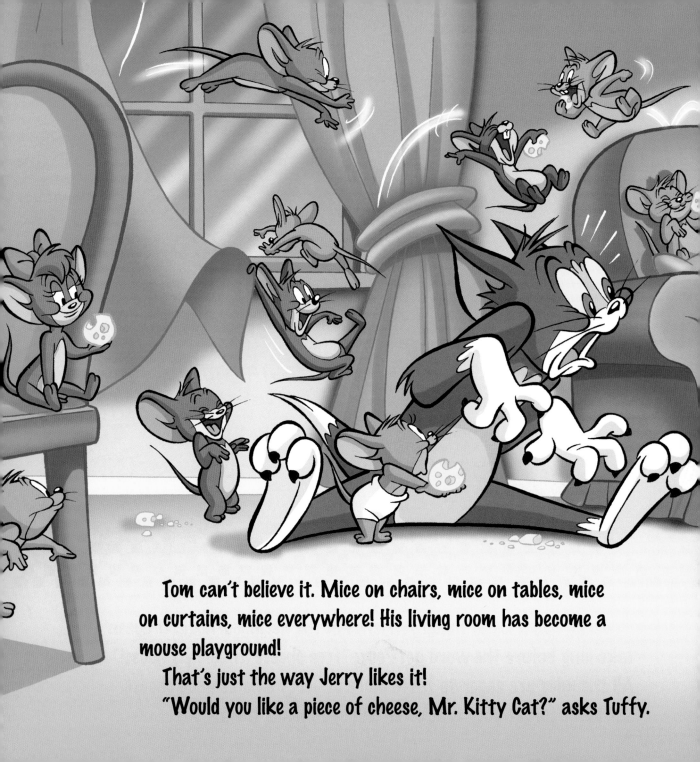

Tom can't believe it. Mice on chairs, mice on tables, mice on curtains, mice everywhere! His living room has become a mouse playground!

That's just the way Jerry likes it!

"Would you like a piece of cheese, Mr. Kitty Cat?" asks Tuffy.

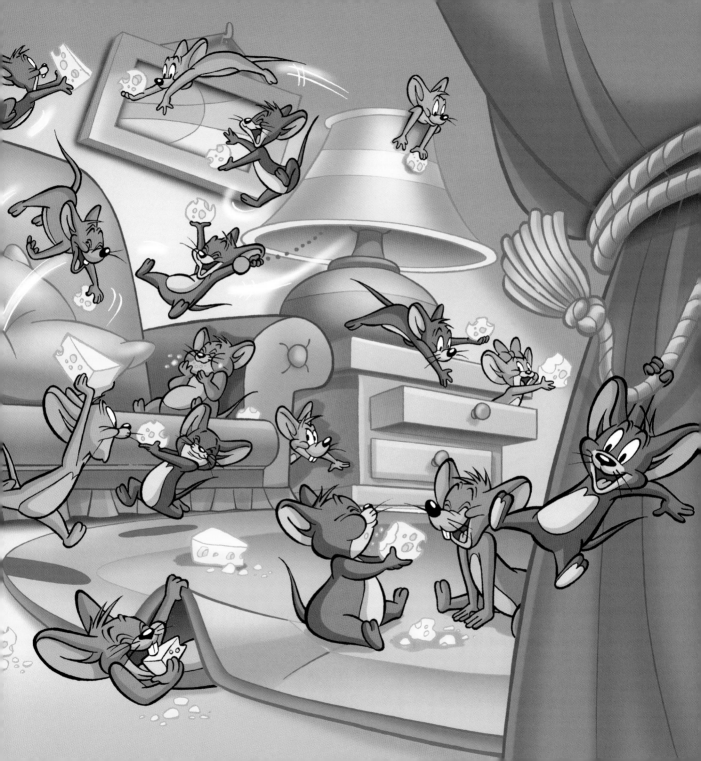

Mice are not supposed to be chasing cats ... but they do at Tom's house! Now Tom is the one being chased, and he does not like it at all. "Meee-Ouch!" he shouts when the umbrella gets too close.
Jerry and Tuffy lead the charge!

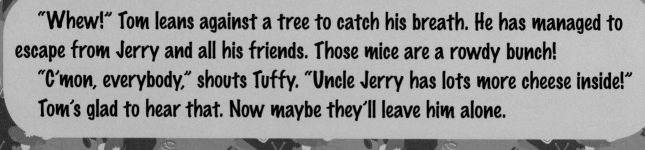

"Whew!" Tom leans against a tree to catch his breath. He has managed to escape from Jerry and all his friends. Those mice are a rowdy bunch!

"C'mon, everybody," shouts Tuffy. "Uncle Jerry has lots more cheese inside!" Tom's glad to hear that. Now maybe they'll leave him alone.

Tom hears some giggling and turns to see his kitty friend watching.

"Why, you showed those big bad mice who's the boss, didn't you, Thomas!"

Tom's face turns red. He didn't want anyone to see this. Especially her! How embarrassing!

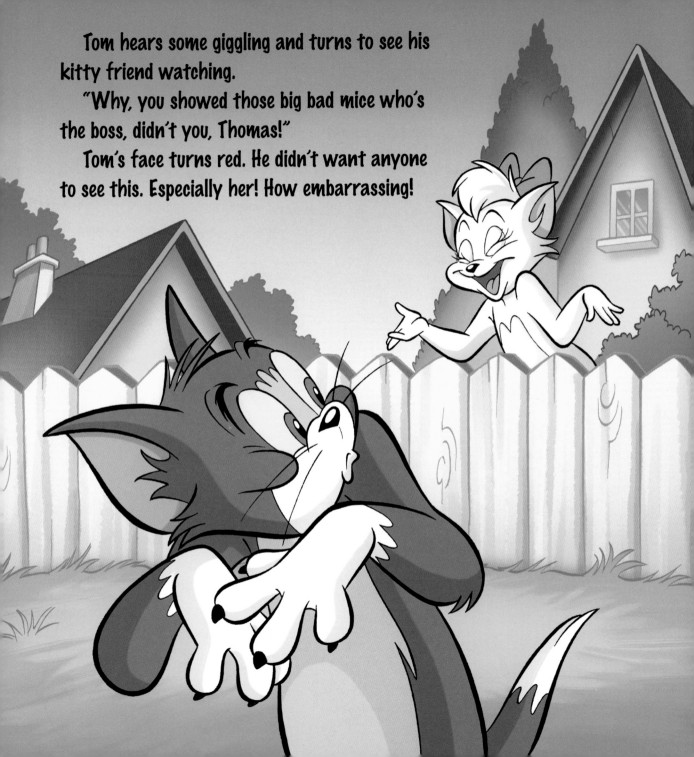

The mouse party is still going strong when Tom returns home. He walks across the room with his groceries, ignoring all the mice.

Tuffy is confused. "Mr. Kitty Cat sure doesn't look scared now, Uncle Jerry."

Jerry nods. He knows that cat is up to something!

Now Tom is cooking! He's boiling milk and stirring pots and ... making cheese?
"I don't get it, Uncle Jerry," says a confused Tuffy. "Cheese is for mice, not cats!"
Jerry knows that Tom is a sly cat.
Homemade cheese would help him catch a lot of mice!

If Tom's going to make his own cheese, Jerry's going to help him.
He and Tuffy sneak over to the stove.
They add sprinkles of a secret ingredient into the cheesemaker.
Tom will be in for a surprise!

At last, the cheese is done!

Now it's time to serve it to all of Jerry's friends. No mouse will be able to resist the homemade cheese of Tom Cat. He'll show Jerry how it's done!

"Huh?" says Tom as he looks around the living room. The mice are gone, and now the room is full of cats! "I'm glad you sent all of our friends home, Uncle Jerry," says a smiling Tuffy. "That way Mr. Kitty Cat's friends can enjoy his catnip cheese all by themselves!"

Jerry and Tuffy watch as Tom runs from all the hungry cats.
Tuffy takes a bit of Tom's cheese.

"Mmmmm! No wonder all of the cats like this," says Tuffy.
"Mr. Kitty Cat makes the best catnip cheese ever, Uncle Jerry!"

Jerry nods. It is tasty! And they can eat all they want while
Tom is busy entertaining his friends!

THE
END